# THE LAST BOOK
# YOU'LL EVER READ

The Last Book You'll Ever Read
Scott Hughes

ISBN: 978-1-948712-27-9

Sinister Stoat Press
Manvel, TX
www.sinisterstoat.com
An Imprint of Weasel Press

Cover by rock_0407
Edited by Jonathan W. Thurston

Printed in the U.S.A.

# THE LAST BOOK YOU'LL EVER READ

## BY SCOTT HUGHES

Sinister
Stoat
Press

*To you*

# THE LAST BOOK YOU'LL EVER READ!

You're curled on the comfy chair next to the crackling fireplace and the den's large window that looks out onto your moonlit back yard. You've been reading Goethe's *Faust* for a few hours, pausing only to add another log to the fire. As the weight of sleep starts to haunt your eyelids, the banging begins at your front door. You flinch and drop *Faust* next to the chair.

"For fuck's sake!" you call out as the thuds continue, like someone is trying to break your door down. "Hold your horses!"

You hurry to the door, which is close to rattling off its hinges from the force of the blows. It's almost 11:00, much too late for a normal visitor. Who is it then? A frantic neighbor? A police officer? An escaped convict fleeing a police officer? You don't have a peephole or a window beside your front door, so you raise your voice enough to be heard over the incessant racket.

"Who is it? What do—" The pounding stops so abruptly that you find yourself practically screaming in your now quiet house. "—you want?"

Odd. You wait, expecting the banging to resume. When

it doesn't, you ask, more quietly this time, "Hello?"

No answer.

You consider going back to *Faust* or maybe even to bed, but you know you'd just lie awake if you didn't investigate outdoors to make sure some lunatic isn't skulking around your yard, perhaps testing all the windows until finding one to easily pry open.

Brandishing a fireplace poker, you unlock your front door and open it a smidge, bracing for a psycho to barge in.

No one.

You definitely heard the whomps on your door. You aren't crazy. Yet no one is out there. Could've been some teens pulling a prank, but no burning paper bag of dog poop sits on your front stoop. You open the door a little wider and stick out your head, half expecting hidden pranksters to chuck raw eggs at you, but nothing appears out of the ordinary. If this were juvenile horseplay, it was rather lazy.

The street is empty save for a few parked cars in front of the other houses. A normal night in a pleasant neighborhood. Just to be sure no one is out there, you say, "Whoever you are, this isn't funny. I've called the cops."

The night air is cool and serene, but a frigid gust rushes past you with the sound of a low voice muttering, "*Liiiieeeessss.*" Somewhere, a dog barks and is answered by another more distant dog. Then, silence descends.

Before closing the door, you think again about the classic flaming bag prank and glance down. Something's on your stoop, just not a fiery sack of excrement. Instead, there's a book, rather large but thin like the storybooks you read as a kid. This one has no title or author's name on its plain, forest green cloth cover. Nothing on it except for a small embossed symbol: two gold circles, one the size of a half dollar above another the size of a quarter, connected by a few intersecting straight and curved lines. To you, it resembles a crop circle.

Using the fire poker, you give the book a quick, light jab as though it's a dead animal you're checking for any sign of life. Then, with the poker you lift the cover. Something is typed on the first page, a couple of short lines, but you can't read the small print unless you get closer. You don't, not right away. This could be a new variation on the old dog poo gag. You'll pick up the book, and underneath will be a squished dog turd or two or maybe even something like a spider or scorpion. You shudder at the thought. You loathe both spiders and scorpions. Anything with more than four legs is, to you, alien. No, *demonic*.

What if this isn't a prank? What if this book's pages are laced with some poisonous powder like those packages terrorists and crazies mail their enemies? But that would be absurd. You have no enemies, at least not any who'd want to murder you. In your entire life, you've had exactly one enemy, Ronnie Barnidge, the Turd King. In third grade, he constantly tormented you by collecting animal feces from the playground and sneaking it back inside to stick under your butt as you sat at your desk or drop it down your shirt before heartily slapping you on the back or mash some into your ham sandwich in hopes that you'd take a bite. Once, in the restroom, he even trapped you in a chokehold while smearing a turd across your lips, saying, "Sissy needs some pretty lipstick," as his cronies Craig Hutchinson and Darrel Stinchcomb cackled themselves to tears. Ronnie Barnidge, however, moved away with his family years later, thank God, and you haven't seen him since.

You raise the book's cover with the fire poker and bend down for a closer look. On the yellowed paper are two typed lines. The first is the title:

*The Last Book You'll Ever Read*

On the next page is a dedication:

*To you*

Your forefinger hovers over the page when you remember the possibility of poison and jerk upright. This must be a prank, albeit one you never heard of and don't see the humor in, although you can see no one hiding behind any of the nearby trees or shrubbery or cars. You can hear no snickering at your expense.

You squat, steady your hand, and flip open the front cover of the book with the poker to inspect the first page. Those two typed lines are still there. You didn't imagine them. You were lying before when you said you called the police. Now, you are seriously considering it.

Then, something like a prickle on the nape of your neck, curiosity perhaps, makes you want to—*have* to—look at the rest of the book before alerting the authorities. You lean down and blow on the page. No dust or any suspicious powder flies off. No immediate danger. You can call the cops in a little while.

Just to be sure, though, you prop the fire poker by the door and retrieve a pair of the latex gloves you keep in the kitchen for handling raw meat. No toxic powder doesn't necessarily mean no toxin at all. Plus, gloves will preserve any fingerprints on the book for when the cops arrive. First, you have to learn what else is written on its pages.

You take one last glimpse around the neighborhood, then hesitate for a moment before plucking the book from your stoop, going back inside, and locking the door behind you.

You return to your reading chair, *Faust* forgotten on the floor, and sit with the green book in your lap. You scrutinize the embossed symbol on the cover, its raised circles and lines, and you remove one of your gloves and trace the design with your forefinger. That same prickling feeling on your neck is now in your fingertip too, like an electric current transferring from the book to your skin.

Then, you realize what you're doing and snap the glove back on. Your heart is racing, hopefully not from some poison now coursing through your bloodstream. You take a few deep breaths and open the book. Again, you are greeted by the menacing yet intriguing title page. Now, in the light of your den, you can see the ink isn't black but actually a very dark red, like dried blood. Another deep breath. You turn the page and start reading: *You're curled on the comfy chair next to the crackling fireplace and the den's large window that looks out onto your moonlit back yard...*

"Mother of God," you say as you flip ahead a few pages and see the exact words you just uttered typed in crimson.

# DARK HIGHWAY

The thumps coming from Tyler's trunk didn't stop until he crossed into Warren County. He needed a drink, something strong enough to knock the hair off his nuts, as his brother Joel used to say, but Tyler couldn't risk stopping, not yet.

Cigarettes. He had smokes. But he was thirsty. Abso-fucking-lutely parched.

*Don't even think about it*, he told himself. *Put it outta your head.* Joel would've told him to send that thought packing. Keep driving, he would've said. Make your Goodyears hum. Under normal circumstances, Tyler would have relished the warm summer air rushing in through the open windows, but these were light-years from normal circumstances.

Now, the cigarettes. Tyler eyed the floorboard, then the passenger seat. He could've sworn he left them on the seat next to him. One hand on the wheel, he leaned over and popped open the glove box. Expired insurance cards, dingy Kleenex, a box of ammo for the Smith & Wesson .38 under his seat. And his Camels.

Tyler held the pack to his mouth to fish out a cig with his teeth. His eyes returned to the road. A few yards ahead, the highway veered sharply to the left.

The car was already off the road before he could jam the brakes. It barreled over the shoulder and across a flat, grassy clearing for thirty feet until it hit a hump of red clay that brought it to a sudden halt. From the trunk came a loud thud. Tyler would have to check on his cargo later. Getting his car back on the road before anyone spotted him was his top priority.

Tyler glowered at the pack of Camels.

*Fuckers nearly got me killed, and not from cancer.*

He popped the hood and got out. About twenty yards from the front of his car was a line of scraggly pines that had shed all their needles, their naked branches like mangled, mummified arms. The forest beyond was somehow devoid of light, as though the setting sun was too repulsed—or frightened—to illuminate it. Tyler couldn't feel any wind, yet the trees' corpselike limbs trembled. Perhaps the darkness was alive, inhaling and exhaling, the branches moving with each breath.

*Looks like they're trying to warn you, bro,* Joel's voice said in his head. *Or lure you in.*

Tyler turned his attention to the car. The engine was still intact, so he closed the hood and wriggled under the vehicle to inspect the chassis. Except for clods of red mud and leaves stuck in all the nooks of the undercarriage, the car was unscathed.

He got to his feet and brushed off his pants. He stepped toward the trunk, stopped, and decided instead to have that smoke after all. He reached through the open driver-side window for the cigarettes. He lit one, closed his eyes, and savored that first earthy, dizzying drag. When Tyler opened his eyes and blew out the smoke, the cigarette fell from his lips.

A young woman stood at the edge of the pines, a languid expression on her face. Della. She was wearing a nightgown, the white silky one where, in just the right light, he could see the slight curves of her breasts and hips underneath. But in this light—the bloody, noxious red of dusk—the gown was like liquid fire enshrouding her body.

"No," Tyler muttered. He felt a jitter in his mind, as if his sanity had been plucked like a guitar string.

Tyler clambered into the car through the window, reaching for the revolver under the seat. His legs flailed in the air. When his hands finally found the gun, he wrenched it free and pulled himself from the car, brandishing the revolver like a crucifix.

Della was ten yards away now.

Tyler leveled the pistol at her and squeezed off two rounds. The reports echoed along the empty highway.

She was still standing, her blank expression unwavering, her gown unblemished.

*I know I hit her, right in the chest.*

Della began walking toward him. Tyler dove headfirst into the car, wondering how she'd followed him.

*She didn't follow me,* he told himself. *She couldn't have. It ain't her. That thing is something else, something that ain't fucking human.*

He turned the ignition, cursing it if it dared to stall, but the car cranked immediately. Tyler threw it into reverse and floored the gas, slinging rooster tails of dirt out in front of the car.

"Goddammit, go!"

He shifted into drive and stomped on the gas again. The tires caught. The car launched. Tyler cut the wheel to the left, then right, trying to steer toward the highway. The car fishtailed, but he wouldn't let off the gas. The car bounced back onto the road. Tyler momentarily left the seat, and his head whacked the roof.

His eyes darted back and forth between the highway and rearview mirror, gauging the growing distance between him and the clearing. Another curve in the road, and the clearing vanished.

*That wasn't her!* Tyler's mind shrieked. *It couldn't have been Della. She's...*

He couldn't finish the thought, so Joel did.

*She's dead, bro.*

Tyler Purdee pressed in the dashboard lighter, careful now to keep his eyes on the darkening landscape ahead, and blindly took a Camel from the pack.

A truck crested the hill. Tyler drummed his fingers on the wheel until the truck passed and its taillights, like malevolent eyes, had faded from sight. The dashboard lighter popped

*—like a thump thump thump from the trunk—*

so Tyler reached for it. His hand trembled. He made a fist to steady his hand, then took the lighter and lit his cigarette. The biting smoke calmed him, though not much. He had to piss, but Tyler wouldn't stop now, not even if Jesus Christ and Elvis were hawking scuppernong wine on the roadside. Not after what he'd just witnessed.

*I imagined her,* he thought. *She wasn't really there. She couldn't be.*

*Oh, she was there all right,* said Joel.

Tyler sucked deeply on the Camel as if he could smoke Joel's voice from his head like smoking a rattlesnake from a gopher hole. It didn't work.

*Real or imaginary, Tyler, you saw her. It ain't important whether or not she was real. The important thing is* why.

*Why what?* Tyler thought.

*Why you saw Della.*

Tyler snorted. *And why's that?*

*Cause of the guilt, bro. Your guilt.*

Tyler shook his head. He would beat his temples with his fists if he could do so without taking his hands off the wheel. Joel's voice had to go. The bastard—Tyler loved his brother, but damn if Joel hadn't been a grade-A bastard—was three years in the ground. Wrecked his car while drunk. Joel Purdee had lost the right to dispense wisdom.

*But the dead never really die, little bro.*

Tyler switched on the radio. Anything would suffice—country, rock, rap, golden oldies. Even a sermon would be dandy, so long as it drowned out Joel.

A couple turns of the knob and the Rolling Stones rose from the static, Mick singing about his nineteenth nervous breakdown. "Here it comes!" he crooned. "Here it comes! Here it comes! Here it comes!"

The cigarette tasted acrid, had burned to the filter. Tyler tossed the butt out the window, glancing in the rearview mirror to see the burst of sparks on the asphalt. He inhaled and held the humid night air in his lungs. He could almost believe that reality wasn't crumbling around him.

The needle on the gas gauge had crept over the red hash

mark, closing in on the dreaded E. He needed fuel, and soon. But he was deliberately choosing his route back to Florida, the highways he knew to be desolate. Few houses. Few cops. Few curious eyes. That also meant few gas stations. He collected his thoughts—a difficult task considering they constantly returned to Della—and figured out where he was. Somewhere between Warrenton and Moses Creek, a stretch of about twenty-five miles of Georgia countryside.

*I'm bound to pass a gas station sooner or later,* he thought.

*No good,* Joel interjected.

*Why not?*

*Think about it, bro. You're at a gas station with other customers around, and even if it looks empty, other customers could show up. You start filling your tank when whaddaya know—thump thump thump from the trunk, for all the world to hear.*

Tyler slapped the steering wheel.

*But,* Joel added, *all you gotta do is go somewhere with no customers, or even the possibility of customers.*

*What gas station won't have any customers?*

*Think, bro.*

Tyler thought. "One that's closed," he said.

*Right as rain,* said Joel.

The pale red full moon followed along overhead. The gas needle was halfway into the red. In Moses Creek, Tyler passed a twenty-four hour BP lit up like a Las Vegas casino, but there were several vehicles at the pumps. As he left town, he saw in his high beams only trees and endless countryside flanking the highway and considered turning back to take his chances at the BP.

He lifted his foot from the gas and was a moment away from pressing the brake and turning the car around when he rounded a bend and came upon a small gas station resembling a log cabin. All its lights were off. A sign on the building read "Roy's Kuntry Store."

"Bingo," Tyler said, pulling over.

He steered the car alongside the two pumps, cut the engine, and stepped out. A staccato of thumps came from the trunk. Tyler tried ignoring it, but in the isolated milieu it sounded like bombs detonating. Tyler pounded his fist on the trunk, hard enough to numb his hand. The noises ceased.

Working quickly, he flipped open the fuel door and unscrewed the gas cap. He tried the pumps on the off chance they had been left on, but they weren't. Tyler scanned the highway. No vehicles. He headed for the store, his boots

—*thumping*—

crunching on the gravel. The front doors were barred on the outside, chained on the inside, and dead-bolted. Country folk weren't so trusting anymore. He peered into the windows and cupped his hands around his eyes, formulating a plan to break into the store to turn on the pumps. He stepped back, hands on hips. A reflection in the glass caught his eye. A white figure on the opposite side of the highway.

Tyler's mouth went dry. He spun around, expecting the road to be empty, hoping that her reflection was only a trick of his tired eyes and unraveling mind.

But Della was there, on the shoulder, her opaque

nightgown clinging to her.

She stepped onto the asphalt. Tyler's leg muscles tensed. His bladder wanted to release.

*The gun*, he thought.

Joel reminded him: *Shooting her's no good. She's already dead.*

Tyler willed his legs to move. They wouldn't. They felt stuck in wet cement. As Della crossed the double yellow line, strength returned to his limbs. He darted to the car and leapt into the driver's seat. He started the car and revved the engine as he fumbled to shift the car into drive. When Tyler finally managed to get the car in gear, the rear tires spat a cloud of dust and gravel, and the car careened onto the highway. Tyler clung to the wheel with throbbing fingers. He knew he should watch the road, but he allowed himself a moment to close his eyes and take deep breaths.

In...and out. In...and out.

His heartbeat slowed.

In...and out.

Then, he opened his eyes. Della was hovering over the hood of the car, only inches from the windshield. She shrieked. The sound shook Tyler's teeth in their sockets. This time his bladder did release, the warmth spreading around his crotch.

She stuck her arms through the windshield—not shattering the glass but passing *through* the glass, like steam through mesh—and her white hands disappeared into Tyler's chest. He felt like an icicle was being hammered into his heart. Coldness spread like vines through his head and stomach and limbs. His chest hitched as he tried to take in air. Panicking, he cut the wheel sharply left, then right. The car pitched side to side, somehow staying on the road. Tyler dropped one hand from the wheel and groped for the pistol, even though he knew it was useless against

—*Della Della Della*—

this *thing*.

His lungs burned from lack of oxygen. His heart slowed. His blood was ice in his veins.

Then, it stopped. She was gone.

Tyler blinked. He could breathe. He checked the mirrors for any sign of her, then accelerated.

He never wanted to feel that again. Her touch had been like—

"Death," he said.

After fifteen miles, the car began to hiccup. It lurched and made chugging noises, jarring Tyler from his shock. The fuel gauge needle was below the red, over the E.

Seven miles later, the hiccups became sputters. Then, the engine died. Tyler shifted into neutral, the momentum carrying the vehicle off the road and onto a grassy tract of land where it rolled to a stop.

Tyler sat motionless, gripping the wheel. He stared at the trees illuminated by his high beams.

"Fuck!" he yelled, throttling the steering wheel and thrashing his head. "Fuck! Fuck! Fuck! Fuck! Fuck!" He pounded the wheel, causing the horn to bleat sporadically. Then, he collapsed onto the steering wheel and buried his face in his arms.

*What now?* he thought. *What the hell now?*

*You know what now*, said Joel's voice. *It's over. Out of gas, bro. End of the highway.*

*I didn't mean for it to happen*, he thought. "It just happened," he mumbled. "I didn't mean for it to."

*But it did.*

Tyler wept.

*I'm sorry*, he thought.

*Sorry won't bring back Della. Sorry won't undo this.*

"I'm sorry," Tyler said. "I'm sorry, Della."

He raised his head and turned toward the empty backseat. Toward the trunk.

"I'm sorry, Katie."

*End of the highway, bro. Out of gas.*

Tyler pressed in the dashboard lighter and readied a Camel between his lips. He lit it and took a few puffs, but it made his mouth taste like ash. Tyler flicked it out the window.

He found the revolver between his feet and checked the chambers. Two rounds left. He needed only one. He held the barrel under his chin and began to squeeze the trigger.

"No."

A voice, not Joel's, not inside his head. A woman's voice.

Della's.

She was sitting in the passenger seat. She had Della's pale face, Della's sable hair, but this was not Della. Tyler sensed something else, something shapeless and feral, hidden beneath her skin.

"You don't get to take the easy way out," Della said.

Tyler yanked at the handle, yet the door seemed to be welded shut.

"No, no, no," he groaned. "I'll let her go. Just...please...let me out. Della, please..."

Before he could attempt scrambling through the open window, the thing that wasn't Della cloaked him in its embrace.

Katie Purdee, almost eight, had never been afraid of the dark like other kids. Until now. Yesterday her daddy, whom she hadn't seen in over two months, found her and her mama at the house in north Georgia a church was letting them stay in since they ran away from him. Her mama told her the house was called something special since it belonged to a church, something like partridge or porridge. Her daddy had shown up at the church house and kicked down the front door while her mama was trying to hide her in a closet under some blankets that smelled like a mangy stray dog.

They were yelling at each other, but Katie couldn't tell what they were saying under all the blankets. All she was thinking was how hard it was to breathe. When she heard a loud bang, she froze. She'd heard guns before on TV but never in real life. Then, she was scooped up with the blankets still wrapped all around her, and her daddy was telling her to hush. She started crying because she didn't hear her mama anymore.

Her daddy set her down somewhere and, without removing the blankets, began wrapping her in duct tape like a mummy. She tried screaming, but that made it harder to breathe with the two or three blankets over her head. Her daddy told her to shut the F-word up, so she did.

Something closed over her. A car engine cranked, and everything around her rumbled. Her daddy had put her in a car. She sat up and conked her head. She was in the trunk.

That's when she started kicking, which was hard to do since her ankles were cinched together, but she didn't stop, not for a long time.

Her head ached, and her eyes burned from crying. Katie was pretty sure her mama was dead. Katie prayed, though, that her mama was just hurt really bad—not dead—and that her mama would wake up and find her somehow. Maybe call the police and tell them her daddy had taken her.

Katie thought she'd never be able to sleep again but eventually found herself drifting off, maybe because she was exhausted or because taking each breath was like trying to suck in air through a mouthful of wet cotton balls or because of the oven-like heat baking her in the trunk or maybe all of that, when the car lurched to a stop. Her head smacked against the inner trunk wall hard enough for her to see blue speckles for a minute instead of only darkness.

She heard the gun again. Two shots. Then, they were moving, the car bucking under her and tossing her around like the coins inside plastic water bottles people rattled at the church softball games. Once the ride smoothed out, the highway humming underneath her, Katie found herself sinking back into something that wasn't quite sleep.

"Wake up, Mama," she kept thinking. She'd tried saying it over and over aloud, but that, like her screams, made it hot and harder to breathe. So, instead she said it inside her head like a prayer, to God and her mama.

Sometime later, Katie didn't know how long, the car stopped. She kicked at the trunk. Her daddy thwacked on the car to tell her to quiet down.

This time when the car started, it veered left and right

and left, and Katie thought she might puke. She bit the insides of her cheeks until she tasted blood. The last thing she wanted to do with these blankets taped around her head was throw up. She bit her cheeks until unconsciousness engulfed her again.

Katie dreamed of her mama's face, except her skin was glowing like when Katie held her hand over the end of flashlight. Katie tried to reach out, but she couldn't move, like her arms were stuck in glue. But her mama placed one radiant hand on Katie's cheek. In the dream, her mama said, "Love you, angel. To the moon and back."

Katie woke up. This time, instead of seeing only the complete darkness of blankets shrouding her face inside a closed trunk, she saw sky overhead. It was gray, but she could still make out some faint stars. She sat up. The blankets and tape were under her, cut open cleanly like someone had done it with a huge pair of scissors.

She quietly climbed out of the trunk, afraid her daddy would see her and throw her back in. But she didn't hear him. A pool of early morning fog veiled the ground. The car looked like it was sitting on top of a flat cloud. Katie peeked around the side and spotted the back of her daddy's head propped against the headrest. She ducked behind the car, wondering if she should bolt for the nearby trees. Her daddy hadn't gotten out yet. If she tried to run, though, he might hear her and chase her down.

But somebody had opened the trunk and cut her free. How could that have happened without her daddy knowing? Unless he was the one who did it.

Katie inched around the car. When she reached the lowered driver-side window, she saw him, then immediately looked away. She got only a glimpse, but the image would forever be burned into her brain. His lifeless eyes were open. His head was tilted back, Adam's apple jutting out, cheeks and forehead mottled with shiny blisters. His mouth hung agape in a silent scream and overflowed with gray ashes and crumpled cigarettes, like the glass ashtray he always kept by his recliner.

Now that the sun had started to come up, the stars weren't there anymore and the fog had mostly dissipated. Not far away was a stretch of highway. Woozy from the sight of her daddy, Katie stumbled along using the car for balance. When she reached the trunk, it looked like an open mouth that wanted to swallow her whole. Before it could, she pushed herself away and staggered toward the road. Even though the dawn made her eyes water, she didn't shield them. The light reminded her of how in her dream her mama's skin had shone.

# EVELYN'S COUNTRY DEPOT

Nick steered a truck pulling a flatbed trailer a quarter-mile through a pecan orchard, and finally the house came into view: a two-story cottage, white with black shutters. Next to the house sat a work shed, also white. "Evelyn's Country Depot" was painted on its side in rudimentary letters. A chain-link fence enclosed an acre of the front yard surrounding dozens, maybe hundreds, of various lawn ornaments sculpted from cement. Nick parked outside the fence.

South Georgia didn't care that autumn had arrived. Nick felt more like he was swallowing the sweltering air than breathing it. He removed his blazer and tie and left them on the passenger seat. Sweat patches darkened the armpits of his blue button-up, and a waxy film of perspiration coated his entire body. Nick couldn't wait to get this over with so he could go home and stand in a cold shower for the rest of his life.

Two years ago, Evelyn Odom had borrowed $30,000 to open this lawn ornament business out of her home. She had defaulted on her loan by not making a payment in ninety days, so Nick had begun foreclosure. Since she'd offered her house as collateral, the bank was going to seize it, but at the moment Nick was here to repossess just the lawn ornaments. He had recently replaced a local retiree in a rural bank who had for decades made careless loans. Nick had spent the last few months repossessing everything from cars and farm equipment to a herd of dairy cows.

He unlatched the gate and entered Miss Odom's yard. The humid air now had a tang of earthy rot. A walkway of hexagonal cement cobblestones zigzagged toward the house through the lawn ornaments, which stood in rows like a battalion of soldiers. The first ones Nick passed were the usual mundane fare: jockeys, snails, gnomes, frogs, cherubs, dogs. Closer to the house, the ornaments became more macabre: frolicking devils, deformed gargoyles with boney wings, imps with mischievous eyes, and monstrosities with Cheshire grins of long cement teeth. Some appeared new, but many had grown freckles of moss.

*Who'd ever buy such crap?* Nick thought. *And why in the hell did the bank loan her the money to start this turd factory?*

Just as he was considering saving one of the ornaments to leave on his retired predecessor's doorstep, something to his left moved. He spun around. Only rows upon rows of cement creatures.

As he made his way onto the porch, the creaky boards announced his arrival. The front door had no bell, so he rapped loudly, then waited. He knocked again, this time calling out, "Miss Odom, this is Nick Harper from Waterston Bank! Miss Odom?"

Nick hoped she wasn't home. He could take his time loading the lawn ornaments and be on his way without her hovering over him.

A wrinkled female face appeared in the window beside the door. The rest of her was hidden by dingy, flowery curtains. Based on how low her head was, the woman wasn't even five feet tall unless you counted her curly wisps of yellowish hair. Her rheumy eyes scrutinized him through the smudged glass.

"Evelyn Odom?" he said.

"Yeah?" she snapped. For such a diminutive woman, she had a fairly deep, forceful voice. It was like a bullfrog croak coming from a Chihuahua. A thin brown dribble of snuff spittle leaked from the corner of her scowl.

"Nick Harper from Waterston Bank. I'm afraid we have to repossess your...lawn ornaments."

"My statues?"

"Yes, ma'am. You've defaulted on your loan. We've made repeated attempts to contact you through certified mail, but you haven't responded."

"You ain't takin' my statues," she said, "or my house."

"Your house is a separate matter, ma'am. I'm just here for the lawn ornaments." Then, he added, "I'm sorry, but it's out of my hands now."

"The hell you say! You ain't takin' what's mine, you sumbitch!" Brown droplets flew from her mouth onto the windowpane.

"Miss Odom, I'm taking the lawn ornaments. If you interfere, I'll have to call the sheriff. I don't want that, Miss Odom. Do you?"

Her watery eyes narrowed. "Get gone, you goddamned shyster, if you know what's best!" Her face disappeared behind the curtains.

Nick turned to begin loading the flatbed, and several of

the lawn ornaments were blocking the pathway. If Evelyn had a friend here, things could turn dangerous. Another loan officer at the bank had told him he was once shot at while repossessing a guy's boat.

Nick rolled up his sleeves, descended the steps, and hurried along the walkway to the statues, as she'd called them, where he began to move aside the ones in his way. How a little old lady moved these heavy things about, he couldn't say.

The more of them he moved, the more there seemed to be in front of him. At first there'd been half a dozen blocking the path. Now, fifteen or twenty of them stood on the walkway.

"What the hell?" Nick said. He wiped his rolled sleeve across his dripping forehead. The heat, exertion, and paranoia made his eyes pulse in their sockets with each heartbeat.

He glanced back at the house. The pathway behind him was now congested with the cement curios. Had one of them, a gnome, just blinked? Nick closed his pounding eyes and pressed his fingers against his eyelids.

Without warning, a flaring pain, like a white-hot spike, shot through his leg. Nick fell to his knees, clawing at his calf. Something was sticking out of it. He yanked out the object—a chisel, covered in his blood. He instinctively applied pressure to the wound, the blood between his fingers as thick and sticky as the air around him.

The lawn ornaments had encircled him. In their small cement hands were pick hammers, pointed stone-carving tools, mallets, and more chisels. Others carried sticks and rocks. The swaying pecan branches overhead cast a network of veiny shadows over the ornaments as they came toward him with the stiff, jerky movements of a marionette. Flecks of quartz on the statues glinted in the patches of hellish sunlight.

Nick stood, his calf singing with new pain, and was pelted with sticks and rocks. As they stoned him, the statues mimicked laughter, although no sound came from their cement throats. When he collapsed, they mimed cheering and applause.

Nick tried fending them off, but they were numerous and quite powerful despite their dwarfishness. They jabbed him with sticks and chisels, beat at his hands and chest and face with hammers, and bound his hands and feet with wire. They propped him up on his knees, and the mob of lawn ornaments before him parted. Several gargoyles marched forward, carrying pails over their heads. Something gray sloshed over the pails' sides.

A cherub gripped handfuls of Nick's hair and snapped back his head, and an imp, leering, forced a rusty funnel into Nick's throat. It tasted dirty and metallic. He gagged. He tried to scream, but only gagged more. He twisted his hands until the wire cut into his wrists. He bucked and seized, but the bonds didn't break.

The statues restrained him with their stony hands and began to pour wet cement into the funnel. It went down his throat and into his stomach, but instead of hardening into a concrete tumor, it spread like gritty roots throughout his body.

The pails kept coming. The lawn ornaments continued to slop this living cement into the funnel and down Nick's throat, pail after pail after pail until his skin began to split like sausage on a grill. Blood and wet cement leaked then gushed from the open wounds, a scarlet-and-slate slurry that began to cocoon his entire body.

The statues finally removed the funnel from his mouth, but the cement had already hardened enough so that Nick couldn't move. Somehow, even though his eye sockets felt full of concrete, he could still see. He stared at the pecan branches and blue sky until Evelyn Odom's face appeared over him. She showed him a wooden mallet and steel chisel in her splotchy hands.

"Told you to get gone," she said. Nick could hear her despite the cement clogging both ears. "Let's see... What should I make you into?" She pressed the chisel's tip to her chin. "I know. A plump housecat. Ain't made one of them in quite a while."

Evelyn placed the chisel against Nick's rigid cheek, tapped the handle with her mallet, and began to carve.

# eXhaurio, Inc.

Harvey Einbinder opened his front door expecting a mailman—or perhaps a UPS man wearing those silly brown shorts—to greet him, but there was no one. Only a cardboard box, three feet on each side, with "eXhaurio, Inc." lettered in yellow on the sides. He'd heard a knock, so where was the person who delivered the package? Harvey stepped out onto the stoop and peered both ways down the deserted street. He eyed the box, then bent over and wrapped his chubby arms around it, nearly throwing out his back as he tried to lift it.

*What's in here,* he thought, *lead weights?*

Once more, he tried picking it up but succeeded only in ripping the seat of his pants. Then, he dragged the box into his house.

For years, Harvey had wanted a computer, but being neither technologically savvy nor financially blessed, he'd never considered himself in a position to purchase one. They became cheaper by the day, it seemed (Harvey could remember when a single computer took up an entire room), but still out of his price range.

Then one night, battling insomnia, he'd lain on the couch staring zombie-eyed at the television. Around four a.m., as sleep began tugging at his eyelids, a commercial came on that caught Harvey's attention.

"Are you tired of expensive computers that constantly crash and get choked down with viruses?" the actor exclaimed as zealously as an evangelical pastor. In fact, he quite resembled one as well: he wore an immaculate pinstriped suit, his hair was plastered to his head, and his animated face was caked with too much makeup, even for someone on TV. To Harvey, the man looked fake, not quite right somehow, like George Hamilton or a mannequin magically come to life.

The actor continued: "Are you sick of buying the most up-to-date PC, only to have it become obsolete within six months?"

Harvey propped himself on his elbow.

"Now, thanks to eXhaurio Computers, Incorporated, for a limited time you can own your own personal computer FOR FREE!"

"Malarkey," Harvey muttered.

"eXhaurio PCs are self-updating and will never become obsolete! They will never crash and are totally immune to viruses, spam, and hackers! eXhaurio PCs come internet ready—no modems or cables! And the best part—they're ABSOLUTELY FREE! You won't pay a single red cent!"

To emphasize this claim, a giant penny filled the screen—Honest Abe staring regally in profile, unaware that he was being used posthumously to hawk computers—with a red X covering it. The penny disappeared, and other letters joined the red X to spell out the company's name—

eXhaurio, Inc., with a little *e* and capital *X*.

"Friggin' scam," Harvey said, but he continued to listen.

The fake man reappeared. "Supplies are extremely limited, so call now! 1-800-555-X-I-N-C. That's 1-800-555-9462. Call now, while supplies last!"

The actor was replaced by the company's name and the flashing phone number.

"Suckers born every minute," Harvey mumbled before finally nodding off.

The first thought to pop in his head when he awoke hours later was of eXhaurio's free computers, but he suppressed the urge to call their number. Nothing in life was free. Nothing worthwhile, anyway.

As Harvey went about his day, changing the blade on his push mower and cutting his back yard, his thoughts meandered back to eXhaurio, Inc. and their supposedly free computers.

*Self-updating,* the man had said, *immune to viruses, internet ready, and the best part... they're ABSOLUTELY FREE!*

By the time Harvey had finished the lawn, he'd convinced himself that no harm could come from calling the toll-free number to see indeed if it was a scam—calling for investigative purposes, not as a purchaser.

Surely, they'd want something: a credit card number for "insurance" or "security reasons," his driver's license number, social security number, a small (translation: *large*) one-time convenience charge, a donation to Greenpeace, a pledge that he'd peddle ten computers to his friends, relatives, or coworkers. Something. If anything, they probably had a phone system like 911 dispatchers that would save his name, address, and phone number into their database, catalogue the information so they could sell it to telemarketers. Those bastards weren't going to make cent one off of Harvey Einbinder. No, in his fifty years he'd learned one thing: Nothing ever came free. There was always a price.

*But it's at least worth a call,* whispered a voice inside Harvey's mind, the voice that belonged to the pasty-faced actor from the commercial. *People get things for free all the time, Harvey. You've just never been one of those privileged people. Well, now you can be, Harvey. Now you can be.*

Harvey held the phone in his sweaty hand dotted with a confetti of grass clippings. He dialed the number—it was easy enough to remember—and held the receiver to his ear. Instead of ringing, he heard a series of clicks on the other end. Then, a recorded female voice answered.

"Thank you for choosing eXhaurio Computers, Incorporated, for your home PC needs," she said dryly. "At the tone, please leave your full name and home address, and your eXhaurio PC will be delivered in three to six days. Thank you."

At the beep, Harvey said nothing. His mouth opened and closed soundlessly, like a fish struggling for its dying breaths out of water. Then, he hung up the phone.

"Gotta be a scam," he said to his empty kitchen.

He took a V8 from the fridge, drank half of it, and burped loudly.

"Has to be a scam. I don't know how, but it is."

Harvey drained the rest of the V8 and burped again.

*Don't be a paranoid simpleton, Harvey.* That voice again. *Be a risk-taker. Those are the people who get things for free, who get the red-carpet treatment.*

"What the hell. It *could* be free."

He seized the phone and hit redial. The same clicks, same female voice, same recorded message. But this time, he spoke after the tone. He left his name and address and hung up before an operator could break in to inform him that he had to enroll in at least three participating program offers to receive his free computer.

"Damn thing'll probably never come," he said.

But it had, and now it sat in a box in Harvey's den. He didn't own a desk, so he wrestled a foldaway card table from the hall closet, dusted it off, and set it up—along with a chair from the kitchen—in the den by a power outlet. He cut the box's packing tape with his house keys and folded back the flaps. Then, with the care of an archaeologist unearthing the remains of an ancient civilization, Harvey removed a layer of bubble-wrap and a layer of Styrofoam before reaching the computer. He struggled to hoist it from the box with no luck. It was heavy as hell. Harvey's job as a part-time maintenance man at Telfair County's middle school required a fair share of heavy lifting, so he knew when to say screw it and go for the hand trucks, only he had no hand trucks at home. So, as if easing someone who's fainted to the ground, he gingerly laid the box on its side and slid the computer out onto the floor. It wasn't like the sleek machines that Harvey had seen on other commercials or in store windows—they had computers now called notebooks that were the size of, well, notebooks. The eXhaurio PC was boxy and cumbersome, as if the designer had given no thought to its aesthetic appeal.

*No wonder it's free*, thought Harvey. *It's so damn ugly. And it's probably been used before, or made from recycled parts.*

He grunted.

On closer inspection, its front panel had a power button, a CD drive, and a slot for 3 ½ inch discs. Below this was a small silver sticker that read "Carver Model" followed by a series of numbers.

With great effort Harvey managed to push the computer under the card table. The monitor, which wasn't nearly as heavy, he placed on the tabletop. Rummaging inside the box for instructions or warranty information or the owner's manual proved fruitless. Harvey scooped out the remaining bubble-wrap and Styrofoam from the box and found only the keyboard and mouse.

Setting up the computer couldn't be too complicated, Harvey thought. It wasn't like he had to build the thing. But crawling under the card table was difficult. Harvey was no small man, and not so young, either. As soon as he got to the floor, his shin splints flared and his tight face throbbed as blood rushed to his head. His gut, which made him appear as though he'd swallowed a bowling ball, hung out from under his T-shirt.

Connecting the machine's components was a breeze. The monitor, keyboard, and mouse all plugged into the computer's back panel. And the computer itself had only one cord, for the power outlet. Harvey plugged it in. The computer lurched and emitted a shrill bleat, like a piglet getting chomped on the rear by its mother. Harvey jumped, smacking his head on the underside of the card table, and scooted back into the pile of Styrofoam and bubble-wrap.

"Jumping Jiminy Jesus!" he said, getting to his feet, his shin splints now secondary to the bright pain in his head.

He'd clocked himself hard enough to make purple splotches swim across his field of vision.

Harvey inched toward the computer as he would a cornered animal. Maybe, he overloaded the power circuit, he thought, and blew the outlet. But the computer's power light was still on. The monitor blinked to life, and letters appeared across the black screen:

GOOD DAY, MR. EINBINDER!

THANK YOU FOR JOINING THE EXHAURIO FAMILY!

"How's it know my name?" Harvey asked no one. Then, it occurred to him that the company must've programmed his name into the computer prior to shipment. As he slid the chair over and sat down, the message was replaced by a blue background filled with various icons.

"Ha!" Harvey said.

A tiny man, a cartoonish caricature of the gentleman from the commercial, strolled onto the screen. *"Hello, Mr. Einbinder! I'm your personalized guide to your new eXhaurio computer, but you can call me Sid. If you would like to begin the tutorial, please press the Enter button."*

Harvey scanned the keyboard, found it, and pressed it.

*"Very well,"* said Sid. *"Let's get on with the tutorial, shall we?"*

Over the next hour, Harvey remained at the computer becoming acquainted with the basics of the machine and its programs, how to use the mouse, how to navigate the internet, and much, much more. Once the tutorial was done, Sid said that if Harvey ever needed assistance, to click the special icon—a miniature version of Sid's face—at the bottom right of the screen.

*"Happy computing!"* Sid exclaimed. He waved and ambled off the screen as if heading to his digital home and digital family for a quaint digital dinner.

Harvey double-clicked on the internet icon. He had never used the internet before. He'd known of it, of course—he didn't live in a cave—but he'd never seen it for himself. He started by perusing sports sites, skimming through the news on how the Braves were faring in the division series. He hadn't kept up with them much in the past few years. Harvey wasn't a baseball man. Football, now there was a game. Chet Merkin, a guy Harvey worked with at the school, once told him that football was prose and baseball was poetry. Harvey preferred prose. Poetry was for fairies and the French. Harvey skimmed the baseball webpages, then searched for news on the Falcons, even though he preferred college ball. A link on the Falcons' page led him to a site devoted to his favorite team—the Georgia Bulldogs. Harvey's idea of a Saturday afternoon well-spent was watching the game muted on TV while listening to the commentary by Scott Howard on the radio.

Hours later, Harvey had visited sites for hockey, basketball, NASCAR, motocross, soccer, and even lawnmower racing.

His stomach croaked. Harvey glanced at his watch. Past four a.m. His eyes ached deep in their sockets. He was hungry—*starving*, in fact—but also nauseated, probably from staring at the monitor. Leaving the computer on, he stumbled through the darkling house to the bathroom. He fumbled with stiff hands through the medicine cabinet, knocking plastic bottles into the sink, until he grasped the antacid tablets. He munched four of them and swallowed the chalky paste. He tried to force out a belch, then popped two more tablets.

His bleary mind could only form simple thoughts: *Bed. Sleep.*

The phone woke him. Harvey shuffled into the kitchen, the phone still ringing. He picked up the receiver.

"Hello?" he said groggily.

"Harvey?" A man's voice. Familiar.

"Yeah. Who's this?"

"Tom Simmons, Harvey. What happened to you this morning?"

Agitation in the voice, which didn't surprise Harvey. Tom Simmons was the Assistant Principal of the middle school and one of Harvey's bosses. Harvey was supposed to go in to work this morning. The clock over the stove showed 3:15 in the afternoon.

"I, uh..." He nearly admitted to oversleeping. "I got sick. Fever, throwing up. I'm in a pretty bad way." Harvey felt thirteen again, faking an illness to weasel out of a test.

"Well, you should've let someone know, Harvey." Harvey could tell from the flatness in Simmons's voice that the man knew he was lying. "Come in Thursday morning. We've got new lockers that need to be installed."

"Sure thing, Mr. Simmons."

Harvey hung up the phone before Simmons could continue. No work until Thursday meant nearly two whole days with the computer. He went to the den, carrying with him a bucket of leftover fried chicken from the fridge.

The monitor was blank, except for this message:

I'VE GONE INTO SLEEP MODE, MR. EINBINDER. PRESS ANY KEY TO RESUME.

Harvey tapped the space bar.

Like a vulture, Harvey had picked the chicken bones clean. He still was hungry. His stomach growled again even though he'd already eaten six pieces, so without taking his eyes off the computer screen he reached over to fish another drumstick from the grease-stained bucket. His hand hit the bucket and knocked it off the table, spilling bones and soggy fried bits across the floor.

"Aw, dammit," Harvey said. He glanced back at the monitor, at his game of solitaire, then got to his hands and knees to clean the mess. As he scooped up the strewn bones and bits of fried skin, he noticed an uneaten thigh between the computer and the wall. Harvey retrieved it, tossed it into the bucket, and saw something he hadn't noticed before. Something that hadn't *been there* before. A purple cord the width of his pinky extended from the back of the computer to the wooden floor. No, *through* the wooden floor.

"What the..."

Harvey leaned in for a closer look. There was now a small hole in the floor, just wide enough for the purple cable to fit through. Powdery sawdust lined the lip of the hole, reminding him of how carpenter bees had made holes in his lawnmower shed.

Harvey touched the cord. Something was moving, like water coursing through a pipe, beneath its rubber tubing.

"Christamighty, what is this?"

Harvey stood and gaped at the computer and the cable for some time. He dug a flashlight from a kitchen drawer and started for the backdoor when his stomach rumbled.

Despite the chicken he'd wolfed down, he felt like he hadn't eaten in days, so he rummaged through the slim pickings in his fridge until he found half a pack of hotdogs toward the back. He hadn't the slightest inkling of how old they were, but at the moment he didn't care. He took one out and chomped it in two bites. Then, he ate another and another. As he opened his mouth to devour a fourth, his thoughts returned to the purple cable, so he put back the hotdogs and headed out the backdoor with the flashlight.

The crawlspace entrance was on the west side of his house, so he'd have to shimmy twenty or so feet under the house along the ground to reach the area beneath the den on the east side. He removed the wooden panel that covered the entrance and shined the flashlight into the crawlspace. Nothing but darkness, dirt, and spiders. Maybe a mouse. Nothing that bothered Harvey. He hunkered to step through the opening, then scooted along on his hand (his other grasping the flashlight) and knees. Cobwebs tickled his nose—Harvey didn't mind spiders, but having their webs stick to his face was damn annoying—as he spotted the lavender cable stretching from his floorboards overhead straight to the ground. Harvey touched the cord. It was as taut as a guitar string, with the same sensation of running water beneath the rubber exterior.

Harvey pulled at the end of the cable closest to the ground, but it remained snugly in the earth. Harvey plucked it like a harp string. Where did it go, and who the hell had put it there? Or had it *grown* like a root from his computer into the ground?

Harvey chuckled nervously. *Nah,* he thought. *That's crazy.*

He stared at the cable for a minute, panting from all the clambering along the ground, then exited the crawlspace.

Back in the den, a new message was on the blank screen:

DO NOT TOUCH THE CABLE, MR. EINBINDER.

When he saw the computer, numbness spread in Harvey's stomach, like someone was holding an icepack to his genitals. He tapped randomly at the keyboard until the message disappeared and the normal background returned. Harvey sat and tried to steer his thoughts away from the purple cord.

*—it bored its way through the floor like a worm and dug itself into the ground lord only knows how deep and to where christamighty where—*

He didn't even want to try to rationalize its sudden manifestation. It was one of those things that would drive you batty if you tried to figure it out. Best not to dwell on it.

*It's back there,* Harvey thought. *So what? It's not hurting anything.*

As he rested his hand on the mouse, he noticed the icon in the bottom right corner. The one that resembled the face of the digital guide, Sid. Harvey clicked on the icon. Sid moseyed onto the screen, a vampiric grin on his face.

*"How can I be of service?"* he asked. *"Please type a word, phrase, or question into this box."* Sid held up one of his hands and a white, rectangular box appeared there. He looked like a waiter carrying a large white tray. A cursor blinked in the box, so Harvey typed "PURPLE CABLE" and hit Enter.

Sid tapped a finger on his chin as if probing the depths of his own computerized brain to recall the information.

*"Sorry,"* he said pleasantly, *"no matches."*

Harvey typed "PURPLE CORD" and hit Enter.

Sid thought. *"Sorry, no matches."*

Harvey tried again: WHAT IS THE CABLE COMING OUT THE BACK OF THE COMPUTER?

*"Sorry, no matches."*

He offered Sid dozens of phrases and questions relating to the cable, but after each attempt Sid would cheerfully reply that sorry, there were no matches.

Harvey gave up and clicked on the face icon. Sid waved goodbye before leaving the screen.

"They said no cables," Harvey grumbled.

Harvey tried to sleep, but in bed he couldn't stop thinking of all the things he was missing. He was connected to the entire world now. Harvey had never smoked or done drugs—he drank occasionally but was hardly what you'd call a "drinker"—but now he knew how smokers and druggies and alcoholics felt while jonesing for their next fix. So, he'd forsaken sleep and returned to the computer.

Around nine a.m., Harvey's phone rang. He knew who was calling, so he didn't answer. It rang again at nine-thirty and once more at ten. Then no more. He was supposed to work this morning, to install new lockers. No doubt Mr. Simmons had been calling to tell Harvey to shag ass and get to the school. Maybe the last call was to inform Harvey he was out of a job. That was fine. Harvey had seen plenty of ads on the internet for jobs he could do from home on his computer (WORK FROM HOME! BE YOUR OWN

BOSS! USE YOUR PC TO MAKE MILLIONS!). No longer did Harvey have to answer to the Tom Simmonses of the world.

Harvey felt too weak to leave the house. He was hungry. No, *famished*. Drained. Standing for more than ten minutes made him feel woozy, so he stayed parked in front of his eXhaurio PC most of the day, occasionally venturing into the kitchen to root through the stale chips and moldy bread in his pantry. Harvey needed groceries. He'd eaten nearly everything in his house and still couldn't fill his stomach. He'd found sites on the internet where you could order groceries and have them delivered to your doorstep, but for some reason none of the companies would deliver to his town. McRae was too small, Harvey guessed. Canned corn and smelly sandwich meat would have to suffice. Harvey munched on these, not really tasting them, as he stared at the computer.

At dusk a searing pain shot through Harvey's head, like he'd sucked down a cold drink too fast. The pain was momentary but intense. He winced, stood, and staggered on shaky legs to the bathroom for an aspirin. As he closed the medicine cabinet, he caught a glimpse of his reflection. Harvey poked his cheeks, which were speckled with stubble. He'd always been overweight and was used to the flabby jowls that normally stared back at him from a mirror. Now his cheeks were flat, almost sunken. His eyes were yellow orbs surrounded by puffy, purplish skin.

Harvey grunted and looked down. His stomach, too, appeared *lessened*. He hooked a thumb into the waistband of his pants and tugged out. They were roomier than a few days before.

*Now, how'd I lose weight sitting in front of that computer?* he wondered. *And I've been eating like a pig at the trough, too.*

"Huh."

He popped two aspirin and headed back to the den, and as he did so he happened to glance behind the computer. What he saw there didn't fully register until he sat down and thought, *Is that purple cord bigger?*

Harvey knelt beside the PC—kneeling wasn't as troublesome now with fewer inches around his middle— and peered at the cable. Two days ago, it had been the width of his pinky. Now, it was wider than a garden hose, and sluggishly it expanded and contracted like the sides of a napping dog. Harvey reached for the cord, then froze, remembering the message that had appeared on the computer's screen: DO NOT TOUCH THE CABLE, MR. EINBINDER! Unknown to Harvey, the same message was there again, repeating enough times to fill the screen. But Harvey's attention was solely on the cable. He wrapped his fingers around the cable and nearly recoiled from its moist, spongy texture, and for a split-second the cable stopped pulsating, as if it had *noticed* him.

"This ain't right," Harvey said. "They promised no cables, so this shouldn't be here."

With both hands, he gripped the cord and yanked hard. No luck. Harvey turned the computer around so that its back faced him, and then braced his feet against it and pulled the cord again. Still, the cord didn't come free, not even a quarter of an inch.

Harvey cursed and released the cord. He marched from the den, returning a minute later with a pair of bolt cutters he had "borrowed" from work, where he used them to cut padlocks off lockers. He stood over the computer and held the open blades over the purple cord. Snip. The bolt cutters sliced through the cable like scissors through string cheese. Red fluid hemorrhaged from the severed end of the cord as it writhed on the floor like a beheaded snake or a nightcrawler impaled on a fisherman's hook. Gagging, Harvey darted to the hall closet and snatched down as many towels as he could carry. He hurried back into the den, and just before he threw the towels over the whole mess his eyes fixed on the cable once more. It had stopped squirming but continued to spurt red into a spreading puddle.

*—my god it's bleeding it's spouting blood all over my floor it looks like i've murdered someone—*

Fortunately, his gorge had settled.

"Must be some kind of computer oil," Harvey reassured himself.

The power light on the computer's front panel was no longer on, and the monitor was black (with no messages), reflecting Harvey's sallow face back at him. He tapped the monitor. Static crackled as his fingertips touched the screen. He pressed the power button repeatedly. Nothing.

"Come on," Harvey pleaded. "Work, dammit!"

Pushing aside the clump of goop-soaked towels, he unplugged the power cord from the wall. He braced himself for the computer to make a noise as he plugged it back in, but the computer made no sound. And it still had no power.

In the kitchen, Harvey called the 800-number from eXhaurio's commercial and heard the monotone female voice telling him to leave his name and address to receive his free PC, but there were no instructions for contacting the company or customer service about a problem. Harvey hung up the phone and went out back where he'd tossed the eXhaurio box. He searched every square inch of the cardboard, thinking the company might have printed a different phone number on it, but the only writing on the box was the computer's name and model number and "eXhaurio, Inc."

Harvey punted the empty box next to his lawnmower shed and stormed back inside. His breathing had become labored. The den tilted to one side, and Harvey could barely stand. He collapsed onto the couch and within minutes was snoring.

Knocking at his front door. Harvey opened his eyes. The light in the den was still on, but outside the sun had long since set. Harvey looked at his watch—just after midnight.

Another knock.

"Don't get your panties in a bunch," Harvey huffed, sitting up on the couch. His head felt as if it was squeezed between two boards and bound tightly with duct tape. The knocking continued. Harvey made his way to the door and began to open it. "This better be good. I don't know who you think you are banging on my—"

Harvey's words stuck in his throat. On his front stoop were two men who stood no taller than Harvey's stomach. Their skin was powdery white, like an albino's, which contrasted drastically with their baggy, dark blue jumpsuits, the kind mechanics wear. They reminded Harvey of Count Orlok from the black-and-white horror flick *Nosferatu*: bald heads too large for their bodies; dark, protruding eyes, as if their eyeballs wanted free from the sockets; thin red lips curled into smiles. Their jumpsuits had nametags: apparently, their names were Fingal and Erland.

"Good evening, Mr. Einbinder," Fingal said in a voice both raspy and childlike. "Computer problems, no?"

Harvey nodded, his jaw stupidly hanging open.

"We're servicemen from eXhaurio."

They squeezed past him into the den, Erland carrying a large toolbox. The eXhaurio logo was emblazoned on the backs of their jumpsuits.

Harvey closed the front door. "I didn't call anyone."

The servicemen crouched behind the computer and whispered. They pushed aside the pile of towels and saw the dried red ooze on the floor and the purple cable lying lifeless on the floor. Their bulbous eyes grew even wider. They opened the oversized toolbox, took out two rags, and began wiping up the dried oil.

"I didn't call anyone," Harvey repeated, taking a hesitant step forward.

Fingal looked up at him. "Don't worry, Mr. Einbinder. We'll have your computer working in no time."

"How'd you know it messed up? That cable—"

"Never touch the cable, Mr. Einbinder!" hissed Erland. Fingal shot his partner a contemptuous look, and Erland went back to work.

Fingal turned back to Harvey with a genial expression. "This cable keeps you connected to our network, Mr. Einbinder. If it ever becomes disconnected, we know."

"Why are you here so late?" Harvey asked, eyeing the coat closet where he'd stashed the bolt cutters. "I cuh... The cable broke almost five hours ago."

"Broke," grumbled Erland.

Fingal ignored him. "We had other house calls before you, Mr. Einbinder."

"Oh." Harvey wondered if the other eXhaurio customers had cleaved their purple cords as well.

"Don't worry, Mr. Einbinder. We'll have your computer in tiptop shape in no time. You should get some rest. You look peaked. Have you been eating?"

Harvey thought what an odd question that was for Fingal to ask, but he heard himself say, "A lot." His eyelids felt suddenly heavy. "I don't have...much food..."

"Sleep, Mr. Einbinder," Fingal said soothingly. "Sleep."

Harvey shuffled to the couch and lay down. He began to drift off while the servicemen worked furiously behind the computer. Just before sleep found him, he heard Fingal say, "Don't touch the purple cable, Mr. Einbinder. Ever. Just enjoy your computer."

When Harvey awoke, the sun was out, and the servicemen were gone. They had cleaned up every drop of the red oil and had even washed, dried, and folded the towels Harvey had draped over the mess. The towels weren't even stained. In the kitchen, Harvey found several bags' worth of groceries on his counter and in his refrigerator. *That's nice of them, I guess,* he thought. He returned to the den and inspected their work. The purple cord, which had returned to the width of Harvey's pinky, was reconnected to the computer. They'd done such a skillful job that he couldn't see the seam where they'd patched the cable.

*They probably gave me a whole new cord,* he thought.

He was relieved now that he knew the cable's purpose—to keep him connected to eXhaurio's network, whatever that meant. He switched on the computer's power as he sat at the card table. The PC hummed to life, and instantly the sensation of being plugged into the world bloomed in Harvey's brain.

Before the regular icon screen appeared, a message flashed briefly on the blank monitor:

GOOD MORNING, MR. EINBINDER! WELCOME BACK!

"Good morning," said Harvey.

Harvey spent the next three days at the computer, only leaving the den to grab something to eat from the groceries the servicemen had left him. Then, something changed. One evening, after eating a frozen dinner he didn't bother to microwave, Harvey sat at the computer and stared at the monitor. He didn't touch the mouse or keyboard, didn't go onto the internet or play any games. He only stared. For eighteen straight hours, he gawked empty-eyed at the screen, his only movements the slight rising and falling of his chest as he breathed. In his mind, however, he was still playing hearts with people from around the world, checking his email account for new messages, and searching for nude pictures of Madonna. Late that night, he slunk off to bed.

The next day, he did the same. And the next day. And the next. He slept little, and despite consuming all the food in his kitchen, he'd lost nearly thirty pounds. Harvey felt hollow, but a different part of him—the part that was connected—felt alive and fulfilled, but only when he sat at the computer.

The computer began to make sounds. Squishes, squeaks, thumps, and throbs. Sounds of contentment, like the purring of a housecat.

Clusters of fierce thunderstorms had settled over most of Georgia, knocking out the power to many homes. The storms had yet to reach Harvey's neighborhood but were still causing hiccups in the power all over the state. In the middle of Harvey's daily staring marathon, the den light dimmed, then went out. The computer screen blinked off. The power was out for only a moment, but that was long enough to break Harvey's focus.

"No," he said. "Come on!"

As if obeying him, the den light came back on, as did the computer, which immediately made mucoid sounds again.

"What in the name of Moses..."

Harvey leaned over to listen. Something was moving inside the computer. Something wet. He placed his hand on top of the computer and drew it away quickly. The PC was burning up, hot enough to redden Harvey's palm. Then he saw the purple cord. It was now thicker than Harvey's arm and was clumped and knotted like a snake swallowing too many rabbits. It pulsated, quicker than before, and made Harvey think of an esophagus pulling food into a stomach. An esophagus without a body.

The sight horrified him, but a more grotesque thought occurred to him. All the weight he'd lost, the feeling of emptiness—of being drained—he'd felt. This computer was somehow responsible. It *was* like an esophagus feeding a stomach, and he was the food.

Harvey knocked the computer on its side and, despite its heat, clawed savagely at its corners. He grabbed a screwdriver from a kitchen drawer and used it to pry open one side of the computer. Then, he pulled away the panel. There were no wires or circuits or microchips inside. Instead, he found a translucent sac filled with reddish fluid. The computer emitted a high-pitched squeal. Harvey stabbed the sac with the screwdriver, then tore it open with his hands. Red fluid spilled from the computer, exposing its contents. Harvey turned his head away and wretched.

The computer was filled with organs. Human organs. A heart, a liver, lungs, intestines, a brain—all of them connected by thin strands of muscle tissue. The organs shuddered and sloshed, continuing the piercing whine.

Harvey jabbed at the purple cord with the screwdriver. Red fluid drenched his face and chest and arms. Finally, he hacked the cable in two, and it wriggled on the floor, spilling more redness everywhere. Harvey still couldn't lift the computer, so he hauled it through the den, through the kitchen, and into the back yard. The rain would come soon, so he had to hurry. He ran back into the house, grabbed the monitor and keyboard and mouse, and threw them on top of the computer in the yard. In the shed he found the gasoline can and a pack of matches. As he emptied the can's contents on the computer, Harvey felt the world begin to spin around him. He hoped that he wasn't too weak. He had to stay conscious, only for another few seconds.

He struck a match and tossed it onto the gas-soaked computer.

The world blurred to a hazy gray, and Harvey collapsed. The computer burned.

Harvey opened his eyes. He was back inside his house. Orange dusk light shone through the slits in the window blinds and rained pelted the roof like thousands of knuckles rapping on a tabletop. Standing nearby were the two albino servicemen, Fingal and Erland. Harvey tried to move but couldn't. He was on his couch, his arms and legs securely bound. Harvey struggled against the restraints.

"You shouldn't have done that, Mr. Einbinder," said Fingal.

Harvey looked behind the servicemen. They'd piled together the charred remains of the computer on the den floor.

"What is that thing?" Harvey asked.

"It's your computer," Erland said. "Well, it *was*."

"That's not a computer," Harvey spat. "It's...I don't know what the hell it is, but it ain't a computer. It was feeding off me."

The servicemen smiled. "We know," Fingal said. "It draws your—what would you people call it?—your *essence*."

"Essence?" echoed Harvey. "What for?"

"Not your concern," said Erland.

"Untie me!" Harvey said, squirming futilely to free himself.

"We can't do that, Mr. Einbinder," said Fingal. "We have our orders."

"Orders?" Harvey said. "What are you gonna do?"

"Don't you know?" Erland asked, fighting back a sheepish grin.

"After dark," explained Fingal, "we're taking you with us."

"Where?" Harvey asked.

"To our factory. You're going to become a computer."

Fingal's and Erland's pallid faces contorted into horrid rictus grins. They seemed to glide as they came closer and stood over him. The bindings on Harvey's wrists and ankles tightened as though they were tiny boa constrictors.

"It's an honor to be a computer," said Erland.

Harvey wanted to scream. He tried. All that escaped him was a whimper, but it was lost in the tumult of rain and thunder.

Debbie Johnston was giddy, like a child at Christmas. This was her first computer, and she'd gotten it free. She'd seen a commercial on late-night television and dialed the number that very minute. A week passed, her anticipation bubbling over like an unwatched pot on the stove. Tonight, just after dark, she'd heard her doorbell and ran to answer it. Expecting to meet a delivery man at her door, she found only a box with "eXhaurio, Inc." on its sides.

After much struggling, Debbie decided the box was too heavy for her to drag into her living room. Instead, she flipped on the outside light and retrieved a pair of scissors, intending to unpack the box right there on her porch and carry the different components into her house one at a time.

Debbie sliced the box's tape and opened the flaps to reveal her new computer. She stroked it as if it was the most beautiful thing she'd ever seen. She ran her fingers over its small silver sticker on which was etched "Einbinder

Model" followed by a series of numbers.

"Einbinder Model?" Debbie said. "What kind of name is that?"

The porchlight flickered once, almost like a heartbeat.

# THE COLOR OF NOTHING

Here goes. Hopefully I can write everything I want to say before I'm engulfed by the black.

This morning, like every other, my Corgi Abba yipped at my side of the bed, her way of telling me to let her out unless I wanted the floor to become her bathroom. I rolled over and stared at the empty space Cheryl had occupied every night of our five-year marriage. Except last night. So, I stumbled to the front door, Abba nipping at my heels, and opened it for her. That's when I saw the wall of solid black. *Walls*, actually.

Although my head was pounding and swimmy from the mother of all hangovers, I managed to wobble down the porch steps without losing my balance or the contents of my stomach. The four walls formed a perimeter around my entire house about thirty feet away, almost the exact size of my property. There was a ceiling of black too, thirty feet overhead. I was enclosed in a black cube. Somehow, though, I could see everything—well, everything inside the cube—as if sunlight were still shining down like any other day.

Abba was bouncing, spinning, and barking at the black like it was the mailman or some kids passing by.

"Abba!" I called. "Come here, girl! Now!"

She didn't listen. I couldn't blame her. If I were a dog, I'd be barking at that strangeness too. I staggered across the yard and scooped her up. She stopped barking but continued growling. I carried her back to the door and shut her inside, where she resumed her hysterical barking. The black itself wasn't the only thing troubling me. It was moving. When I first let Abba out, I could see my mailbox. After I put her inside, my mailbox wasn't there anymore.

I crossed the front yard to one of the black walls. It was perfectly flat and smooth like a mirror, only not reflective. I've been trying to think of ways to describe its color besides *black* since I started writing this down, but I never was the writing type. I always made C's and D's in English. Nothingness? That can't be right, can it? Black is *something*, so it can't also be *nothing*. Or *is* black the color of nothing? All I can say is that whatever this is it's the blackest black. Think of shark eyes or crow feathers or a tar pit, except...those have a shimmer to them that this black doesn't.

I know what you're thinking. (It's weird to address you directly since I doubt anyone will ever read this, but I felt the need to write it down. To pass the time, to keep my sanity, to *do* something.) Anyway, I know what you, if there is a you, are thinking. Why didn't I freak out? Why didn't I run in circles and scream like a loon, like Abba? I can honestly say I don't know. I always heard the brain has a way of dealing with unbelievable things, that it releases chemicals that help us not go insane when we're faced with something shocking. Maybe it's my particular brain chemistry, but I'll get to that. Maybe I was just too hungover. My head was already spinning, so if I started raving like a madman I'd puke my guts out.

I found a stick that had fallen from the magnolia tree in my front yard and stood a few feet from the wall. I extended the stick, expecting it to touch the black, like poking any solid surface with a stick. Instead, it disappeared *into* the black. When I pulled it back, it was a few inches shorter. It had been cut clean, as smooth as the wall itself. I stared at the end of the stick. Didn't dare touch it. I tossed it aside and headed back in.

Abba was literally losing her shit. She'd pooped and peed by the door, but I didn't bother cleaning it up. I got my phone from the bedroom and turned it on. No service. It couldn't access the internet either. Neither could my laptop. I didn't have a landline. Does anyone except the elderly have landline phones anymore? If I did, I'm sure it wouldn't have had a dial tone. I tried the TV. It wouldn't come on. Nothing in the house was on. No power. Whatever the black was, it had totally cut me off from the outside world.

Then, a series of thoughts came to me that almost made my knees buckle: Is there an outside world anymore? Is there a universe? Is my house the only section of reality that still exists? Am I the last one left? Well, me and Abba.

But the sunlight. Somehow, sunlight was shining through the black. That's what I believed then. Now, though, I'm sure the black makes its own light. I try not to think about that. What the black is, why it's here. I don't think my brain could handle going down that rabbit hole. One way or another, I don't have to worry much longer. The rabbit hole is coming for me.

I went around checking every light switch and electronic device. Nothing. I fiddled with the breaker box in the garage. Nothing. I fed Abba. I didn't feel like eating. The fridge wasn't working, so I'd have to eat everything in it soon. Funny the things you think sometimes. Here I was, waking up to a box of solid black surrounding my house, and I was worried about sandwich meat spoiling and Breyers mint chocolate chip melting.

I did grab the nearly empty bottle of Jack Daniels from the counter where I'd left it last night, to take a big swig, but when I unscrewed the cap and got a whiff, I gagged. With a DEFCON 1 hangover, the hair of the dog doesn't work. Just makes it worse. I dropped the bottle, flopped over the sink, and vomited. Abba sniffed at the spilled whiskey on the floor, then returned to her kibbles.

I spread a few hand towels over the spill and set the bottle on the counter. That's when I peered out the kitchen window. In the back yard, the black wall was closer than the wall in front of the house had been. For some reason, brain chemicals or hangover or what have you, I was still calm. The black was twenty feet away. It had consumed the gazebo I built a few years ago for Cheryl. I used to wheel my grill out there, and we'd listen to the neighborhood sounds—kids playing, maybe music and laughter from someone's backyard party, Abba barking at one thing or another and other neighborhood dogs answering her. The aroma of sizzling steaks or chicken would waft over us, me with a Jack and Coke and Cheryl with a glass of chardonnay. Good days.

I went outside, circled the house, and saw that the other walls had closed in. The black ceiling looked lower, too. Sometimes in the gazebo, Cheryl played songs on her phone, and suddenly I remembered one in particular. Can't remember who sang it even though Cheryl told me several times. The singer's name sounded weird, the song even weirder. Cheryl loved it. I heard it so much I have the lyrics memorized. Seeing the black made me think of the chorus: *Closing in. I hope that you make it. Closing in. I hope that you find your way.*

I grabbed the magnolia stick from the front yard and approached the black. I didn't poke it into the wall again. I already knew what that did. This time I jammed the stick in the ground like a flagpole half a foot from the black, as a marker.

Back inside, Abba was scratching at the towels like she was making a nest. I shooed her away. She yapped, which she always did after a meal. Cheryl always said Abba's intestines were a direct line from her mouth to her rear. I didn't let her out, though.

I did peek through the front window. The magnolia stick marker was gone. The black was steadily encroaching. At this rate, it would swallow the house—and everything in it—in a couple of hours. Assuming it didn't start to move faster.

I checked my phone again several times, to see if I'd somehow get service. Nope. I did have ten of my favorite songs saved to it, nowhere near as many as Cheryl had on hers, so I sat on the sofa with Abba balled up next to me listening to the Rolling Stones' "Beast of Burden," Stevie Wonder's "Superstition," Fiona Apple's "Paper Bag," Queen's "Radio Ga Ga," Ben Folds Five's "Song for the Dumped" (how appropriate), Bruce Springsteen's "Brilliant

Disguise," Fleetwood Mac's "Go Your Own Way," Snoop Dogg's "Gin and Juice," Radiohead's "No Surprises," and ABBA's "Voulez-Vous" (my guilty pleasure). Screw it. Who am I trying to impress? I straight up love ABBA. No guilt whatsoever. I named my dog after them, for Christ's sake.

As the Stones faded out and the funky drums and clavinet signaled the beginning of "Superstition," I started wondering what, if anything, was happening outside the black. If it hadn't devoured everything else in the universe, were there people gathered around this shrinking black anomaly? Were there news vans? Police, FBI agents, or the military? Cheryl?

Periodically, I checked the black from different windows. Each time, the walls were closer. After one playthrough of my phone's songs, my entire yard—front, back, and sides—was gone. After two playthroughs, the black had made its way to the house.

I picked up Abba—I didn't want her to run into the black when I wasn't watching—and turned off my phone. You get sick of your favorite songs pretty quick if you listen to them over and over, especially if there's unexplained blackness eating the reality around you inch by inch. Besides, it made me queasy to think of listening to those same songs as the black closed in, wondering which one would be the last I'd ever hear.

That's when I considered just walking into it, Abba in my arms. Do the opposite of that old poem: Go gentle into that good night. I don't remember who wrote it. I told you, I wasn't the best English student. Or like that Neil Young song. Out of the blue and into the black. I also considered getting a bottle of something or other from the liquor cabinet, drinking until I—pardon the pun—blacked out, then decided against it. Whatever was coming, I wanted to face it sober. Hungover, yes, but sober.

Instead, still carrying Abba, I fished a pen and yellow legal pad from the kitchen junk drawer. Good thing they were there, or I might've ended up writing this on toilet paper with one of Cheryl's eyeliner pencils. From what I'd seen, the black was creeping in methodically, so I retreated to the centermost point of the house, the guest bathroom. I shut the door and set Abba down. She lay on her side at my feet.

I lowered the toilet lid, sat, and began writing. Why? Why not? As I said, it was a way to keep me from going nutso or committing suicide. Maybe, somehow, whatever I write will survive and end up in someone's hands as a record of what happened inside the black. Sounds preposterous, I know, but no more preposterous than having an unexplained black cube closing in on you. And although I've never been religious, writing might be a way to end this. Maybe this is a test from God, like some Old Testament shit. Excuse me. Old Testament *stuff*. Maybe if I offer a sincere apology to Cheryl, the black will begin to retreat. Possibly disappear.

If you're not my wife, please get this to her. Cheryl Dunham. If it's God or Allah or the Flying Spaghetti Monster reading this, then I'd still like you to get this to her. Your omnipotence should make that easy.

First, Cheryl, I love you and I'm sorry. So sorry. If you're not Cheryl, a little explanation. The quick version. Not sure how much time I got.

I've struggled my entire life with depression. I was

never officially diagnosed. When you've dealt with it as long as I have, you don't need to be. Every few months or so for as long as I can remember, I'll wake up some random morning filled with profound sadness. About what? Everything. Nothing. When it happens, I can't will myself to get out of bed, like all my blood is replaced with lead. I just lie there barely moving, rarely eating, hardly sleeping for a week, sometimes two. Then, poof. Gone. The world feels normal.

It really became a problem in college. I flunked out after one semester. From then on, I couldn't hold a job for more than six months, ten at the most. They don't like it too much when you stop showing up for a couple weeks without a phone call.

When I met Cheryl, things got better for a while. That year and a half when we started dating and first got married was the best of my life. I figured Cheryl had cured me. That's what makes depression such a bitch. Love can't cure it. So, a few months into our marriage, I woke up with the old lead veins, as I call it. Cheryl freaked. She thought something was seriously wrong, like maybe I'd had a stroke. She called 911 when I refused to go to the doctor. Paramedics showed up, took my vitals, and told her everything was A-OK. Physically, anyway.

Cheryl was in nursing school at the time, and she tried helping me as much as she could. I got to give it to her. She tried. My depression would return. She'd beg me to see a therapist. I wouldn't. Then, it'd go away, and we'd forget about it. Pretend to forget, at least. We could do that back then, or believed we could. Cheryl got more persistent when she saw the losing-job-after-job part. In the meantime, she finished nursing school and got a great job. Started demanding I see a therapist. Said medication would really help. I told her the only medication I needed was alcohol and a bit of weed. We fought. She threatened to leave me if I didn't get help. I never believed her. We did this dance for the past few years. I'd have a job, the depression would swoop in, Cheryl would press me to get help, I wouldn't, I'd lose that job, the depression would vanish, and the cycle would start over.

After I got fired from my last job, as a server at a local restaurant, Cheryl said I should go back to school. I reminded her of my shitty first attempt at college. She said I didn't have to try for a bachelor's degree. Anyone who's worked in the restaurant biz knows it's one of Dante's levels of Hell. (Maybe I remember more from English class than I thought!) But I mentioned to Cheryl things I really liked about it, especially watching the cooks. She'd gotten a brochure for the local community college's culinary program. Even though we couldn't afford me going to school, she said we'd make it work. She wanted me to have a career that'd make me happy. I promised I'd try the program. But like love, hope and happiness can't cure depression.

I put off applying to the college for several days. Last week, I woke up with the old lead veins again. Cheryl was different this time. She didn't demand I get help. Didn't fight. Didn't really say anything. Then, last night when she came home from work, she brought something. I was in bed, Abba curled into a furry donut beside me. Cheryl plonked down a large white pill bottle on the nightstand. It had one of those long unpronounceable medication names on it along with a ton of other fine print.

I asked her what it was.

"Your last chance," she said.

"That ain't what the bottle says," I said.

She said the name. She could pronounce it, of course. "It's for depression," she said.

I told her I wasn't going to take it, that I'd heard that shit makes people like zombies. She told me I already was a zombie. I called her a bitch.

"I could get fired for taking those from the hospital," she said. "I could lose my license."

I regret what I said next. Cheryl, if you read this, I really didn't mean it. Really. I can't blame it on anything other than myself for being an asshole.

"Fuck your license," I said. "You always thought it made you better than me. If you were actually smart, you'd be a doctor. Not a goddamn nurse."

Those were the last words I said to her. That I'll ever say to her. Cheryl shoved some of her things in a bag and stormed out. I listened to the car start and drive away, and then the lead in my veins evaporated. You'd think the opposite, but having your wife leave you is an instant cure for depression. Temporarily, at least. I slid out of bed, marched to the fridge, and guzzled a beer. Then another. And another. Then graduated to my old pal Jack. You know the rest.

The black has made its way into the bathroom. It's a few feet over my head. If I stood, it would shear off the top third of my body like it had the magnolia branch. Even though I'm in a closed bathroom with no power, there's still light. That's why I'm sure now the black makes its own light. I can still see. Maybe it wants me to see everything right till the very end. It hasn't come up through the floor yet, though I suppose it will. It has a top. Probably has a bottom. The bathroom door is gone, and the doorknob clattered to the floor, sending Abba into a frenzy. I tried to grab her as she lunged forward and bit at the black. It sliced off the tip of her nose. She yelped, let loose a few dribbles of urine, and hid behind the toilet.

Its movement is so slight I can barely see it. The only way I can tell is because of the lines of grout between the floor tiles. It approaches one line of grout until it swallows another row of tiles, then another.

Never thought I'd spend my last moments on Earth writing while sitting on a toilet. I'm almost done. I'm going to set down the legal pad, pick up Abba, sing to her, and wait to pass into whatever, if anything, is beyond.

There are worse ways to go, I suppose. Other than the fact that I'm on a toilet, this might be the best—a loving dog on my lap and belting my favorite ABBA songs. Dog. Disco. Darkness. Death. I know there's a term for that, for starting words with the same sound. Can't think of it now. Oh well. Gotta go. Time to sing my way into the black.

# THE LAST BOOK YOU'LL EVER READ II

"Mother of God," you say as you flip ahead a few pages and see the exact words you just uttered typed in crimson.

The hairs on your arms stick up like stiff wires. Your brain screams out for you to rip this damned book into the tiniest shreds you can and flush them down the toilet or toss it in the fireplace and burn it to ash. Rid the world of it somehow. Even more powerful than your own brain, however, is the prickling feeling that has spread from your neck and fingertip throughout your body, inside and out. Every fiber of your being—except your brain—pulses with the desire to keep reading.

So you do: *You've been reading Goethe's* Faust *for a few hours...As the weight of sleep starts to haunt your eyelids, the banging begins at your front door... "For fuck's sake!" you call out as the thuds continue, like someone is trying to break your door down...It's almost 11:00, much too late for a normal visitor...You don't have a peephole or a window beside your front door, so you raise your voice enough to be heard over the incessant racket...*

On and on it goes, page after page, precisely describing tonight's events. Instead of flushing or burning the book, you sit rereading the last sentence of the sixth page: *Instead* of flushing or burning the book, you sit rereading the last sentence of the sixth page.

How the hell is this possible? How is this book doing what it's doing? What's on the next page? The one after that? And after that? What's on the *last* page?

All these questions are floating—are screaming themselves—in the remaining sane sliver of your brain not spellbound by this book. The prickling desire is stronger, louder, than your sanity. You aren't in control anymore.

You turn the page. The words there, though, are blurred—the letters like rivulets of wet paint. It's probably from eye strain. You were reading *Faust* for a few hours before finding this book. You take off the latex gloves and rub your closed eyes. You blink several times, massage your eyes again. Then, gloves abandoned, you return to the book. The words aren't blurry anymore. It was your tired eyes after all. Or was it? The seventh page starts with these sentences: *You turn the page. The words there, though, are blurred—the letters like rivulets of wet paint.*

It continues until you reach a sentence that really stands out from the rest: *The words aren't blurry anymore. It was your tired eyes after all. Or was it? Little do you know, this is the last book you'll ever read.*

You slam the book shut. You stare at the cover's crop circle symbol, feel it staring back at you, and flip the book over facedown on your lap. As you eye the back of the book, the prickling desire grows, spreads, intensifies into an itch throughout your body—a lust on a molecular level. You have to know how this story ends.

Instead of returning to where you left off, you do something you've never done in all your years of reading.

You skip to the end. You open the back cover to reveal the last yellowed page's final sentences: *Instead of returning to where you left off, you do something you've never done in all your years of reading. You skip to the end. You open the back cover to reveal the last yellowed page's final sentences. Then the deep red ink once more begins to blur—to run like wet paint, like wet blood. The words are alive, and they are hungry. So very hungry.*

As you finish, the ink begins to blur. No, to *move*. The words, the ink itself, are alive just as the book said. Strands of red fluid squirm up from the page, wind around your right wrist, and begin to dig into your skin.

Finally, you overcome the shock. You scream and fling the book as hard as you can, nearly dislocating your shoulder. The book strikes the wall and lands open, cover side up, on the carpet. For a moment, you're certain you hallucinated the last few minutes. The book is real—you can see it there on the floor—but maybe its pages were tainted with some drug, the effects of which you are now suffering. Time to call 911, to find out what you've been poisoned with and who the hell would do such a thing.

When you stand from your reading chair, the book stands, too. The pages sprout crimson arachnoid legs of ink, each about three feet long. How many legs you aren't sure. Definitely more than four. You aren't about to stand there and count the exact number. Your cellphone is charging in the kitchen, but the front door is closer.

You bolt for the front door. However, you don't have the preternatural speed of whatever this book creature is. To your credit, you almost make it before the tendrils lasso your left ankle, sending you sprawling forward where your face collides nose-first with the door.

You try to cry for help, but the tendrils, legs, tentacles, or whatever they are loop like a noose around your neck and squeeze. There right in front of you, where you left it propped by the door, is the fire poker—your last chance to fight off this thing. When you reach for it, a dozen inky tendrils grab your wrist and snatch your arm back. You hear your bones break before the searing pain engulfs your forearm. The ink crawls under your clothes and up your legs, buttocks, back, and other arm like thin ropes of lava melting into your flesh.

Another cluster of tendrils does what you can't and takes hold of the fire poker. They cast it away, and it clatters against the wall somewhere behind you. Then, hundreds, maybe thousands, of sanguine cords fill your ear canals. They worm into your nostrils and pack your sinuses and mouth and esophagus with their wriggling, metallic heat. You choke out a noise that's more gag than scream, and the slippery blood-eels slither down your throat. You retch, then convulse, but you can do nothing to stop them. They needle through your eyeballs and into the sockets.

You can't read the book's final words, but you hear their whisper despite your burst eardrums, you smell their coppery stench, you taste their acidity on your swollen tongue, you feel their venom in your muscle and gut and groin and brain, and you see their crimson afterimage in your popped eyes:

THE END.

# ACKNOWLEDGMENTS

*For Mom,
the first to read me a story.*

I must begin by thanking the numerous writing teachers I've had over the years. There are too many to name them all, but I have to mention a specific few: Gordon Johnston, Martin Lammon, Judson Mitcham, Ruth Knafo Setton, and Brenda Whitley. If not for their wisdom and guidance, this book would not exist. I also want to thank the editors of the publications in which these stories first appeared: *The Haunted Traveler* ("Dark Highway"), *Lonesome October Lit* ("Evelyn's Country Depot"), and *[silverthought]* ("eXhaurio, Inc."). I owe unending gratitude to my editor, Jonathan W. Thurston, for helping me craft the separate stories I first sent him into this cohesive collection. I would like to thank Sara Pirkle Hughes, who for two decades has been my first and best reader. Finally, to my family and close friends (again, too many to name)—I cannot thank you enough for your support and love. Without teachers and editors, I would not have a book. Without you, I would not be a writer.